P9-DGF-722

3 1192 01164 0008

JPicture Schul.J

Schulman, Janet.

Countdown to spring : an
animal counting book /

OCT

COUNTDOWN TO SPRING!

AN ANIMAL COUNTING BOOK

By **JANET SCHULMAN**

Illustrated by **MEILO SO**

EVANSTON PUBLIC LIBRARY
CHILDREN'S DEPARTMENT
1703 ORRINGTON AVENUE
EVANSTON, ILLINOIS 60201

Alfred A. Knopf ✦ New York

It's spring!

Do you think the children who live here will remember their animal friends on this special day?

10 Ladybugs

crawling

all

around

the

crocuses.

Can you
count them?

9 Butterflies

See them flutter by.

8 Birds

singing cheep, cheep, cheep.

7 Chicks

saying peep,

peep,

peep.

6 Ducklings

noisily quack, quack, quacking.

5 Mice

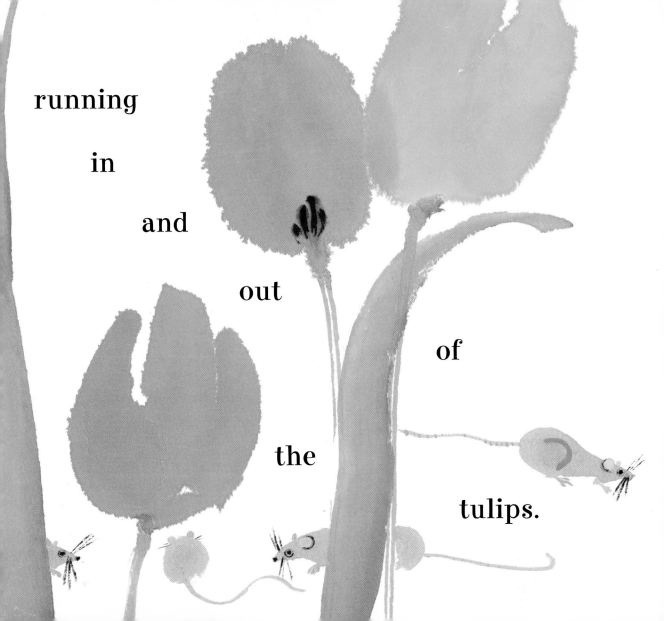

running

in

and

out

of

the

tulips.

4 Bunnies

sniff, sniff, sniffing.

3 Squirrels

scurrying up and down the tree.

2 Foxes

A mother and her baby, creep, creep, creeping.

1 Easter Basket

filled with treats for all the animals.

"Thank you!" said the happy animals.
Now count them all again.

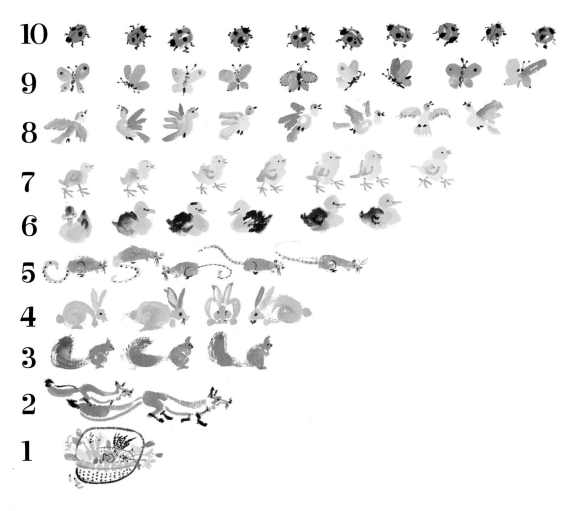

To Ming.
—J.S.

To Janet, the woman of ten thousand books.
—M.S.

THIS IS A BORZOI BOOK PUBLISHED BY ALFRED A. KNOPF

Text copyright © 2002 by Janet Schulman
Illustrations copyright © 2002 by Meilo So
All rights reserved under International and Pan-American Copyright Conventions. Published in the United States
of America by Alfred A. Knopf, a division of Random House, Inc., New York, and simultaneously in Canada by
Random House of Canada Limited, Toronto. Distributed by Random House, Inc., New York.
KNOPF, BORZOI BOOKS, and the colophon are registered trademarks of Random House, Inc.

www.randomhouse.com/kids

Library of Congress Cataloging-in-Publication Data
Schulman, Janet.
Countdown to spring! : an animal counting book / by Janet Schulman ; illustrated by Meilo So.
p.   cm.
ISBN 0-375-81364-0 (trade) — ISBN 0-375-91364-5 (lib. bdg.)
1. Counting—Juvenile literature. 2. Animals—Juvenile literature.
[1. Counting. 2. Animals.] I. So, Meilo, ill. II. Title.
QA113.S389 2002
513.2'11—dc21   2001029465

Printed in the United States of America

January 2002

10   9   8   7   6   5   4   3   2   1

First Edition